THE GODS

OF

OLYMPUS

FOR KIDS

Written by Maria Karra

Edited by Vivian John Stevenson
Illustrated by Samantha Altarozzi

Published by FRESNEL PRESS
12781 Orange Grove Blvd
West Palm Beach, FL 33411

Printed in the United States of America

Table of Contents

1. The Gods of Olympus 2

2. Zeus 8

3. Hera 12

4. Poseidon 16

5. Athena 20

6. Ares 28

7. Aphrodite 32

8. Demeter 36

9. Hephaestus 40

10. Hestia 46

11. Apollo 50

12. Artemis 56

13. Hermes 60

14. Dionysus 64

15. Pluto 68

1. The Gods of Olympus

Zeus   Hera   Poseidon

Athena   Ares   Aphrodite

Demeter

Hephaestus

Hestia

Apollo

Artemis

Hermes

Dionysus *Pluto (Hades)*

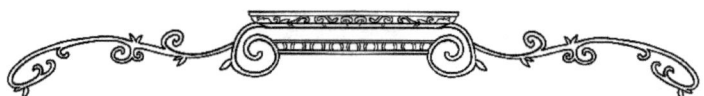

The ancient Greeks believed in twelve principal gods who resided at the top of Mount Olympus, the highest mountain in Greece. From there they ruled over the world and the affairs of mortal men. They were: Zeus, Hera, Poseidon, Athena, Ares, Demeter, Hephaestus, Aphrodite, Apollo, Artemis, Hermes and Hestia.

These gods were descended from powerful beings called the Titans, whose father was Uranus (the sky) and mother was Gaia (the Earth). There was a great rivalry between the Olympians and the Titans, and it plays an important role in Greek myth.

In addition to the twelve main gods of Olympus, there was also Pluto, the god of the underworld. Dionysus, the god of wine and festivity, originally had a minor role, but he asked the other gods for a place on Olympus. Hestia gave him her throne, which is why we sometimes see Dionysus instead of Hestia among the Olympian gods. There were also demigods: children born to a god or goddess and a mortal, whose great feats brought them eternal fame. Examples are Heracles and Achilles.

Each god had specific abilities. For example, Artemis was excellent at hunting, Poseidon could control the seas, and so forth. They fed on ambrosia and nectar.

The gods very often came down to earth and helped or punished people. Despite their powers and immortality, they had virtues as well as faults, just like humans.

In this book we will learn some basic information about each of the twelve gods.

2. Zeus

Zeus was considered the father of gods and of men. He was the son of the Titans Cronus and Rhea, and the grandson of Uranus and Gaia. Zeus's father Cronus (known as Saturn to the Romans) was supreme ruler and very protective of his power. In fact Cronus swallowed all the children born to Rhea because he was afraid that one of them would take his throne, as predicted by a prophecy. That is why Rhea, when she gave birth to Zeus, tried to protect him from her husband. She wrapped a stone in swaddling clothes and gave it to Cronus, who swallowed the bundle believing it contained his newborn son.

Young Zeus grew up on the island of Crete, away from his parents. When he came of age, he rescued his trapped siblings by forcing Cronus to disgorge them. Thus came Hera, Poseidon, Hestia, Demeter and Pluto. Together with his brothers

Poseidon and Pluto, Zeus fought Cronus and the other Titans and took power. He made Poseidon king of the seas, Pluto king of the underworld, and kept for himself the kingdom of heaven and earth.

Zeus is considered the god of light, the sky, lightning, and weather phenomena in general, but also the god of law, order, and justice. His symbols are the eagle and the thunderbolt. He threw thunderbolts whenever he got angry. He is also called Zeus *Xenios* (from the Greek word *xenos* which means 'stranger, foreigner') because he protected strangers and encouraged hospitality. He was married to Hera. Their children were Ares, Hebe, Hephaestus and Eileithyia. Zeus also had many children with other women, which made Hera very jealous. Some of those children were Athena, Apollo, Artemis, Hermes, Aphrodite,

Persephone, Dionysus, Hercules, Perseus, Achilles, and Helen (known as Helen of Troy), among others.

The Greeks worshiped Zeus and considered him a wise and just god who punished the doers of evil deeds and eased the pain in people's hearts. He was believed to be superior to the other gods in both physical strength and rank.

Olympia was a place dedicated to Zeus, and the Olympic Games were held there in his honor. Among the Roman gods he was called Jupiter.

3. Hera

Hera was Zeus's wife. She too was the daughter of Cronus and Rhea, which means she was also Zeus's sister. After dethroning Cronus, Zeus asked for Hera's hand in marriage, which initially she refused. So one day, while Hera was walking in the forest, Zeus transformed himself into a cuckoo and fell at her feet. Hera caressed him and then Zeus took his true form. He was so impressive and powerful that Hera could not resist. She married him and gave birth to Ares, Hebe, Eileithyia and Hephaestus.

Hera was the goddess of marriage, women, childbirth, and motherhood. She also had warlike qualities. In the Trojan War she helped the Greeks and opposed the gods who took the side of the Trojans.

Hera was a very powerful goddess and all the gods respected her. She was the only one who could confront Zeus about his actions or decisions. She is also renowned for being possessive and vengeful. Because Zeus had many children with other women, Hera was very jealous and took revenge not only on those women but on their children too. One of those children was Heracles (whom the Romans later called Hercules), a renowned hero of Greek mythology. Heracles was the son of Zeus and a mortal queen called Alcmene. Hera pursued him from the moment he was born.

Despite her jealousy, Hera is presented in the myths as a model woman: faithful, strong, and intelligent. We often see her holding a scepter, a symbol of her rule as queen of the gods. At other times she holds a pomegranate, a symbol of fertility. Other symbols of hers are the peacock and the cuckoo, which symbolized the coming of spring and the union of Hera with Zeus. To the Romans she was known as Juno.

4. Poseidon

Poseidon was the god of the sea. In his power were also the lakes, the springs, and the rivers. He was the fifth child of Cronus and Rhea and the brother of Zeus, Pluto, Hera, Demeter, and Hestia. He lived in his palace in the depths of the sea with his wife, Amphitrite. Poseidon had many children. Among them were the hero Theseus, the infamous robber Procrustes, and Polyphemus the Cyclops. Poseidon was the patron of sailors and fishermen.

Once, Poseidon tried to seize Zeus's throne on Olympus and become king of the gods. But Zeus saw through Poseidon's plans and banished him. So Poseidon went away and worked with Apollo to build the city of Troy. Poseidon loved Troy, since he helped build it, which is why he sided with the Trojans—and not with the Greeks—in the Trojan War.

Besides being the god of the sea, Poseidon was responsible for storms, hurricanes, and earthquakes. He always held a trident with which he calmed the waters. But if he was angry, he would use his trident to strike the sea and raise huge waves, or to cause earthquakes and volcanic eruptions. Poseidon loved riding his golden chariot on the waves while dolphins played around him. He was also very fond of horses. He domesticated the first horse and was the father of the mythical winged horse Pegasus. That is why one of his symbols is the horse. His other symbols are the dolphin and, of course, the trident.

Poseidon was worshiped in many parts of Greece, particularly in coastal areas and lands bounded by the sea like promontories and islands. The Romans knew him as Neptune.

5. Athena

Athena was the goddess of wisdom and the arts, and also of strategy and war. She was Zeus's favorite daughter. Her mother was the wise nymph Metis, Zeus's first wife. Before Athena was born, Zeus swallowed Metis because he learned from a prophecy that Metis would give birth to a god who would take his throne. Later Zeus began to suffer from headaches, so he ordered his son Hephaestus, the god of metalworking, to help. Hephaestus cut Zeus's head open with an ax, and out came Athena. She was already an adult, wearing armor and a helmet, and holding a shield.

Athena was famed for being wise and clever. On one occasion she and her uncle Poseidon both laid claim to a certain city: each wanted to be its patron. The rest of the gods decided that this honor should go to the one who offered the most useful gift to the inhabitants. So while the people watched, all the gods assembled on a great rock above the city to decide the winner. Poseidon struck the rock with his trident, and immediately a spring of water burst forth (according to another tradition, a mighty horse emerged from the rock). The inhabitants admired the spring but soon realized that its water was salty, like the water of Poseidon's realm, the sea. So the gods decided that this gift was not very useful. Then Athena stuck her spear into the rock, and an olive tree began to grow in that spot. The gods considered this gift to be much more useful than Poseidon's salty water, since it could provide the city with food, oil, and timber.

Thus, Athena was declared the winner. She became patron of the city and named it "Athens". The Athenians loved the goddess Athena very much and dedicated a temple to her on the rock above them. The rock of course is the Acropolis, and Athena's temple is the Parthenon (from the Greek word *parthenos*, meaning 'virgin'), because despite having many admirers the beautiful goddess of wisdom never married or had a consort.

Athena played a very important role in two great stories ('epics') called the Iliad and the Odyssey. Though very ancient, they are still enjoyed today, and many films and stories are based on them. Paris, a son of Priam the king of Troy, was judge in a beauty contest between Athena, Hera, and Aphrodite, and he chose Aphrodite as the most beautiful goddess. Athena got very angry at him, so later during the Trojan War she sided with the Greeks. The war, which was partly caused by this beauty contest, is described in the Iliad.

What happened after the Trojan War is told in the Odyssey, which recounts the ten-year journey of the Greek hero Odysseus (called 'Ulysses' by the Romans) back to his island kingdom of Ithaca. Athena also did everything she could to help Odysseus reach his homeland to reunite with his wife and son, and reclaim his palace and throne.

Other heroes who were protected and helped by Athena include Achilles, Diomedes, Telemachus (son of Odysseus) and Perseus, to name just a few. In fact, Perseus, with Athena's help, killed a famed monster known as the Gorgon. This hideous creature with a woman's body and snakes for hair was originally a beautiful mermaid named Medusa, with whom Poseidon fell in love. But the two offended Athena by disrespecting one of her temples, so Athena transformed Medusa into something frightful. Anyone who gazed directly upon her would be turned to stone. However, Athena gave Perseus a marvelous shield that shone like a mirror, and with it he succeeded where others had failed. By looking at Medusa's reflection in his shield, Perseus was able to approach and kill her. He then offered her head to Athena in tribute. That is why we see Medusa's head carved on Athena's shield, which is called Aegis.

Although Athena was the goddess of war, she was also the goddess of peace and the arts, such as sculpture, architecture, and painting, among others. Many festivals were held in her honor. The most important was the Panathenaea, which was celebrated every year with sports and music competitions.

Athena's symbols were the owl, which represented knowledge and wisdom; the helmet, representing war strategy; and the olive tree, which stood for peace, friendship and – of course – the goddess's gift to the Athenians. To the Romans she was known as Minerva.

6. Ares

Ares was the god of war, violence and hatred. He always wore armor and carried weapons. He was the son of Zeus and Hera; the Romans knew him as Mars. Ares liked to terrorize people. He always tried to find reasons to make people fight and hate each other. They say that his servant once forgot to wake him up at dawn, so Ares transformed him into a rooster to punish him. Since then, the rooster crows every day at dawn.

All the gods despised Ares, except Aphrodite, who found him brave and fascinating. This, of course, made her husband, the plain-looking metal smith Hephaestus, quite jealous. Even Zeus, Ares's father, disliked him because this warlike son was always aggressive and only cared about fights and battles.

In the Trojan War, Ares took the side of the Trojans, which is why he often came into conflict with Athena, who supported the Greeks. Although both Ares and Athena were gods of war, there was a huge difference between them: Ares represented violence, aggression, and bloodshed, while Athena represented strategy and intelligence. In other words, Athena believed that in order to prevail one had to use one's mind and design a clever plan, while Ares was impulsive and had no patience for tactics and plans, believing that wars could be won by brute force alone.

The Greeks won the Trojan War with the famous ruse of the Trojan Horse (and the help of the goddess Athena). This left Ares's fellow gods questioning his abilities as a god of war.

Ares's symbols were the snake, the spear, the shield, and the torch.

7. Aphrodite

Aphrodite was the goddess of beauty and love. She was born out of the foam that bubbled up when the blood of Uranus fell into the sea during a fight with his son Cronus. The sea foam is called *aphros* in Greek, so the goddess was named Aphrodite. Another myth says that Aphrodite's father was Zeus and her mother was Dione.

Aphrodite married the god Hephaestus, who was very ugly. She did not choose him herself; it was Zeus and Hera who forced him upon her because Hephaestus had blackmailed them.

Admired by all gods and men, Aphrodite was rivaled in beauty only by Hera and Athena. Each thought she was the fairest, and this caused jealousy between them. One day, the goddess Eris proposed to settle the arguments by holding a beauty contest between the three. Zeus wisely refused to be the judge, and Paris, the prince of

Troy, was appointed instead. Eris gave Paris a golden apple to present to the winner. Each contestant promised something in return if she won. Aphrodite, who understood men, told Paris she would give him the most beautiful woman in Greece. So Paris chose Aphrodite and awarded her the golden apple.

In those days, Greece's greatest beauty by far was Helen of Sparta (who later became known as Helen of Troy), a daughter of Zeus himself. Everyone knew that Helen was already married to King Menelaus, but this detail didn't trouble Aphrodite. Later, when Paris visited Menelaus in Sparta, he fell in love with Beautiful Helen (as she was known), and Helen with him. With the goddess's help, Paris stole Helen and took her home to his city of Troy. Menelaus considered this a great insult, so with his brother, King

Agamemnon of Mycenae, he organized a Greek expedition to Troy to take Helen back. Thus began the Trojan War.

The little winged god Eros was Aphrodite's son. He held in his hands a bow with golden arrows and flew invisibly among people. When he wanted to make someone fall in love, he shot an arrow into their heart. Aphrodite also had a son with her fellow god Hermes; this child was named Hermaphroditus because he combined the qualities of both his parents.

Aphrodite was worshiped in various places, especially at ports, where she was considered the patroness of sailors. Her symbols were the dove, the apple, the myrtle, the rose, and the winged Eros. Aphrodite and Eros were both worshipped by the Romans, who knew them as Venus and Cupid, respectively.

8. Demeter

Demeter was the goddess of agriculture, nature, and the seasons. Her father was Cronus and her mother Rhea, which means she was the sister of Zeus, Poseidon, Hera, Hestia, and Pluto. Demeter was the patroness of farmers. She taught people how to cultivate the land. She also gave them very useful and nutritious grains such as rye, corn, wheat, and barley. These grains are called *demetriaca* in Greek, from the name of the goddess. Similarly, our word *cereal* comes from the name Ceres, which is how Demeter was known to the Romans.

Demeter and Zeus together had a daughter, named Persephone. One day, Pluto, the god of the underworld, saw Persephone and fell in love with her. So he seized her and secretly took her to his kingdom of the dead, called Hades. Demeter pined terribly for the missing Persephone. She left

Olympus and began to wander among mortals, looking for her only daughter. In her wandering she stopped a while in the city of Eleusis, where in sympathy she helped a mother and child.

Because of Demeter's grief, the land fell into heavy winter and became barren. Plants and seeds stopped growing, and animals died. People suffered from hunger and diseases. When Demeter learned that her brother Pluto was the one who had stolen Persephone, she was furious. She immediately went to Zeus and asked for his help. Zeus decided that Persephone should spend six months of the year on earth with her mother, and six months below ground with her husband. So, according to the myth, when Persephone is with Demeter it is spring and summer and everything blooms, while during the six months that Persephone is with Pluto in Hades it is fall and winter. This is how the ancient Greeks explained the four seasons.

Demeter's many qualities earned her several nicknames, including Demeter *Thesmophorus* ('bringer of order') because her crops made civilized life possible. Women and farmers especially worshiped Demeter, and organized many festivals to honor her. Two were very important. One was the Thesmophoria, an autumn planting celebration in which only married women could participate. The other was the Eleusinian Mysteries, which related to her time in Eleusis. Both festivals involved secret and protected knowledge, about which we know very little today.

Demeter's symbols were the ear of corn, the pomegranate, and the crane bird.

9. Hephaestus

Hephaestus was the son of Zeus and Hera. He was the god of fire, metallurgy and volcanoes. He had his workshop in a cave on Olympus. There he melted metals and made tools, weapons, and other metal objects.

According to legend, he was very ugly compared to the rest of the gods. Indeed when Hera gave birth to him on Olympus, she felt great shame and anger at having produced such an ungodly looking baby, and threw him into the sea. As he fell, Hephaestus hit his foot on the rocks of Lemnos, an island in the Aegean Sea, and consequently limped for the rest of his life. Another tradition says that Hephaestus's leg was badly hurt after Zeus threw him from Mount Olympus, because once when Zeus quarreled with Hera, Hephaestus took his mother's side. Homer, on the other hand, says that Hephaestus was born lame, and this was the reason why Hera rejected him.

Whichever version is most accurate, according to all of them, Hephaestus was lame and ugly. The other gods often mocked him for his rough looks and handicap. Hephaestus was very hurt by their behavior because although he seemed tough, he was in reality very sensitive. In general, Hephaestus was a kind-hearted god, always happy and very pleasant. At the feasts of the gods on Olympus, he poured wine and made everyone laugh with his jokes.

But Hephaestus also had his vengeful side. When one day he learned that Hera had thrown him into the sea when he was a baby, he decided to take revenge on her. So he made a golden throne to which he attached invisible ropes and offered it to Hera. When Hera sat on the throne, she got trapped and could not escape. None of the other gods could help her.

In her desperation, Hera promised Hephaestus to grant him any wish of his. He announced in front of Hera and the other gods that he wanted the goddess Aphrodite as his wife. All of them were stunned. They could not imagine the most beautiful goddess together with the ugliest god. But Hera and Zeus realized that they had no choice, so they agreed to give Aphrodite to Hephaestus.

Another version of the myth says that Zeus gave Hephaestus Aphrodite as his wife to please him, because when Zeus was fighting the Giants, Hephaestus made thunderbolts in his workshop, and so helped Zeus win the battle.

The symbols of Hephaestus are the hammer, the anvil, the ax, tongs, and fire. The flames and smoke rose above his mountain smithy, and he sounded like thunder as he forged the hot metal. To the Romans he was known as Vulcan, which is of course where our word 'volcano' comes from.

10. Hestia

Hestia was the protector of the home and family, and played a very important role in the daily life of the ancient Greeks. In the center of each house was a circular altar where a flame always burned in Hestia's honor. In all the festivals, people dedicated the first and the last sacrifice to Hestia. They also offered her the first crops from the fields.

Hestia was the first child of Cronus and Rhea, and therefore the oldest of the twelve gods of Olympus. She was the kindest, the most peaceful, and the most altruistic of all the gods. She never took part in wars. All the gods respected her. She was the one who often reconciled them when they argued with each other. She always tried to ensure there was peace, love, and respect among gods, and that each one was happy. A typical example is that when

Dionysus, who was a lesser god, asked to be given a throne on Olympus, Hestia gave him her own throne so that the gods would not quarrel with him. That is why, among the twelve gods, we often do not see Hestia but Dionysus instead.

In people's houses, and in the center of every city, there was a hearth with a flame that never went out. It was from here that the ancient Greeks took the sacred flame and carried it to each new colony. In this way they symbolized the bond between the two cities. People also believed that the common hearth not only of Greece but of the whole world was the one at Delphi, where the navel of the Earth was located. If Delphi's flame ever went out, it was a very bad omen. Only the sun could bring it to life again to burn untainted as before.

The main symbol of Hestia is, of course, fire, which is why she usually holds a torch in her hand. Her other symbols are the scepter, and a bough with fruits. She was called Vesta by the Romans and equally revered by them.

11. Apollo

Apollo was the god of music, light, the sun and divination, as well as archery, inspiration, poetry, male beauty, and medicine. He lit the world when he drove his fiery sun chariot across the sky behind four great horses.

One of Apollo's children was Asclepius, who is considered the father of medicine and the first physician of mankind. Because Asclepius cured all diseases, Pluto complained to Zeus that souls had stopped going to Hades. So Zeus killed Asclepius by striking him with a thunderbolt.

Just as Aphrodite was the most beautiful goddess, Apollo was the most handsome god. He was tall and fit, with long blond curls that framed his blue eyes. Young people dedicated their hair to him when they cut it for the first time.

Apollo was the twin brother of the goddess Artemis. Their father was Zeus and their mother was Leto. Legend has it that Leto was desperately looking for a place to give birth to her children while Zeus's wife Hera, full of jealousy, chased after her. No place welcomed Leto: everyone sent her away her for fear of angering the queen of the gods. Leto eventually found refuge on the free-floating island of Ortygia which, lacking a fixed position, could not easily be found by Hera. So Leto safely birthed Apollo and Artemis there. Afterward, Zeus (or, according to another tradition, Apollo himself) anchored the island in place and named it Delos, which means 'clear and bright'.

Like other Olympian gods, Apollo also participated in the Trojan War. Together with his sister Artemis he took the side of the Trojans against the Greeks. He was the main helper of the

Trojan Prince Hector, famous opponent of the Greek hero Achilles.

Apollo was the god of divination, which means using mystical abilities to interpret and foresee events (a person with this skill is called an oracle). A Temple was dedicated to Apollo high on Mount Parnassus at Delphi. From there the will of Zeus was revealed to the people – first through Apollo himself, and later through a priestess called the Pythia. Also called the Oracle of Delphi, this priestess sat on a golden tripod to receive visitors. Many climbed the mountain to consult the Oracle on their fates and fortunes.

Apollo, as the god of music, was leader of the nine Muses. At the festivals of the gods on Olympus, he played music on his lyre as the Muses danced and sang.

In addition to being a sun-god of many virtues, Apollo was also the god of death, which he generally dealt with his bow. In the Trojan War he caused great harm to the Greeks by sending a plague into their camp. When Calchas, the soothsayer of the Greeks, went to seek an oracle about the cause of the plague, he learned that "the god who shines like light is the one who brings darkness and death". This shining god of course could only mean Apollo.

Romance for the gods was often complicated, and Apollo was no exception. Once he fell in love with a beautiful nymph named Daphne, who did not want him in return. When Daphne was young, the god Eros had pierced her with one of his arrows, but not the kind that made someone fall in love. By mistake, he had sent her an arrow that caused her to never love anyone. So, even though Apollo was handsome and strong, Daphne avoided him. One day Apollo started chasing her and she begged the gods for help. The gods took pity on Daphne and transformed her into the plant that has ever since carried her name, which in Greek means 'laurel'. From then on, Apollo always wore a laurel wreath on his head and never forgot the girl he loved.

The symbols of Apollo were the lyre, the sun, the laurel, the bow, and the arrow. The Romans also knew him by his Greek name, although he was sometimes called Phoebus by them.

12. Artemis

Artemis was the twin sister of Apollo. She was born on the island of Ortygia, later called Delos. Her father was Zeus and her mother was Leto.

Artemis was the goddess of hunting and archery. Fittingly, as her twin brother was the god of the Sun, Artemis was the goddess of the Moon. She was born before Apollo, and even helped her mother give birth to her brother, even though she was still a newborn. That is why she is also considered goddess of childbirth along with Hera. She was the protector of small children and of animals.

A goddess of wild places, Artemis spent most of her time in the woods where her favorite pastime was hunting. Her aim with bow and arrow was infallible, never missing the mark. She was always accompanied by her hounds and by the

Nymphs, who were young and beautiful maidens. On her walks in the woods her favorite deer would never be far from her side.

Artemis was very beautiful, very intelligent and very dynamic. From an early age she knew what she wanted and was firm in her decisions. Zeus admired her for her dynamism and determination, and always did any favor she asked of him. From a young age she had decided to remain a virgin and pure forever. She devoted herself to nature and hunting, and like Athena, she was indifferent to love and marriage.

Artemis was very strict and never forgiving. When she was very angry at someone, she would shoot them with her deadly arrows. She punished those who did not respect animals and plants and who killed them for no good reason. She also punished those who did not respect her purity and modesty. On the other hand, she had a weakness for children and young people who maintained their innocence. Girls dedicated their hair to Artemis the first time they cut it.

Artemis was worshiped throughout Greece. The ancient Greeks admired her and sacrificed rams, oxen, and bulls on her altars. One of the seven wonders of the ancient world was the temple of Artemis in Ephesus, which took 200 years to build.

The symbols of Artemis were the moon, the bow, arrows, the stag, the lion, the hare, and many other animals. To the Romans she was Diana, the huntress.

13. Hermes

Hermes was the messenger of the gods, that is, he conveyed the will of the gods to the people. That is why he was considered the god of communication and diplomacy. He also accompanied the souls of the dead to the underworld. He was the son of Zeus and the nymph Maia. Maia was one of the Pleiades, the daughters of the titan Atlas who held up the sky on his back.

Hermes was one of the most likeable and familiar gods because his character had many human traits, not only positive but also negative: he was cunning, lied a lot, and often tried to deceive people and the other gods. From a very young age he was mischievous. A few minutes after his birth, he stole Apollo's oxen. Apollo, as the god of divination, immediately identified the culprit and was enraged. Quick to appease this anger, Hermes made a lyre from a turtle's shell and a sheep's intestines and gave it to Apollo. It was the first lyre in the world. Apollo was enchanted by its melody. He forgave Hermes and moreover rewarded him with a scepter (called "caduceus") by way of thanks. This is the scepter we often see in ancient Greek sculptures and illustrations, with two snakes around it (and which many confuse with the rod of Asclepius, which is entwined by one snake only).

Hermes was the protector of shepherds and flocks; his sacred animal was the ram, which is why he is often depicted with one on his shoulders. Wayfarers enjoyed his favor, and columns carved with his figure were common features at crossroads. Statues of Hermes were found in gymnasiums because young athletes, especially wrestlers, also had his protection.

Merchants, and trade and commerce in general, looked to Hermes as their patron god as well.

Hermes was not only first in craftiness, stealing and deceiving: he was also the patron of thieves and the unscrupulous. Many householders erected a column carved with Hermes's figure in front of their houses, in order to obtain the god's favor and ward off any thieves.

The symbols of Hermes were the caduceus, the winged sandals which he always wore, the tortoise (from whose shell he made the first lyre) and the ram. To the Romans, he was known as Mercury.

14. Dionysus

Dionysus was the god of the grapevine and wine. He was also the patron of the theatrical art. He was the son of Zeus and the mortal Theban princess Semele. He was the youngest god of Olympus and the only one with a mortal mother (the rest were born to goddesses or titans). He was married to Ariadne, princess of Crete.

Dionysus is often not counted among the Olympian gods, for example in Homer's epics. According to one myth, he came to be considered an Olympian god when Hestia gave him her place.

Dionysus loved wine and fun. He taught people to grow vines and make wine from grapes. In his honor Greeks organized many great festivals, such as the Dionysia, where the people celebrated by getting drunk, singing and dancing.

Dionysus was also the god of madness. When he wanted to punish someone, he sent madness into his or her mind.

His symbols were the grapevine, climbing ivy, and the drinking cup. His name among the Romans was Bacchus.

15. Pluto

Pluto was the god of the underworld, that is, Hades. At first, the word "Hades" referred to both the god and the place (i.e. the underworld) but later only to the place. Pluto was the son of Cronus and Rhea. He had three older sisters, Hestia, Demeter and Hera, and two younger brothers, Poseidon and Zeus.

After Zeus came of age and freed his siblings from Cronus's stomach, he and his fellow gods claimed power from their parents and their uncles, the Titans, in a series of battles called the Titanomachy. The Cyclops, who had been imprisoned by Cronus, helped the young gods by gifting them valuable weapons: to Zeus they gave the thunderbolt, to Poseidon a trident, and to Pluto a helmet that made him invisible whenever he wore it.

The gods were victorious, and Zeus became ruler of heaven and earth, Poseidon became ruler of the sea and every liquid element, and Pluto took over the underworld. Pluto's wife was Persephone, whom he stole from her mother Demeter in a cunning way.

Pluto ruled over the souls of the dead, and was enraged whenever one of his subjects tried to escape and return to life. But there were a few heroes who famously succeeded: Heracles, Orpheus, Theseus, Odysseus, and Aeneas.

To reach Hades, the dead entered the boat of Charon, who was the ferryman of Hades, and crossed the river Acheron. Charon charged one *obol*, a coin which the relatives placed under the deceased person's tongue. The destitute, and those who had no relatives or friends to pay the fare, remained forever on the banks of the Acheron. On the opposite bank awaited Cerberus, a terrifying three-headed dog, the guardian of Hades.

Although Pluto was an Olympian god, he lived in his dark realm Hades, which is why we do not see him among the twelve gods of Olympus. He was terrifying, fierce, and strict, with a dark personality and no mercy. He was, however, considered very fair and impartial. When the Greeks prayed to him, they would pound their hands on the ground to make sure he heard them. Black animals, such as sheep, were sacrificed in his honor. He had an impressive black chariot which was pulled by four black horses (the opposite to Apollo). In his kingdom he sat on an ebony throne.

Pluto's symbols were Cerberus, the bident (a spear similar to Poseidon's trident, but with two points which symbolized life and death), the cypress, the narcissus lily, and the key.

The Romans also called him by the same name, which came about in this way: the underground world where the god had his kingdom was also where prized minerals lay buried. Thus, from the *wealth* of the earth came the name *Pluto*, which in Greek means 'wealth and riches'. This is the origin also of the modern word 'plutocrat'.

www.ingramcontent.com/pod-product-compliance
Lightning Source LLC
Chambersburg PA
CBHW072232190626
46809CB00017B/1896